PROFESSOR ASTRO CAT'S

ATOMIC ADVENTURE

A JOURNEY THROUGH PHYSICS

WRITTEN BY DR DOMINIC WALLIMAN & BEN NEWMAN
ILLUSTRATED BY BEN NEWMAN

FLYING EYE BOOKS
LONDON – LOS ANGELES

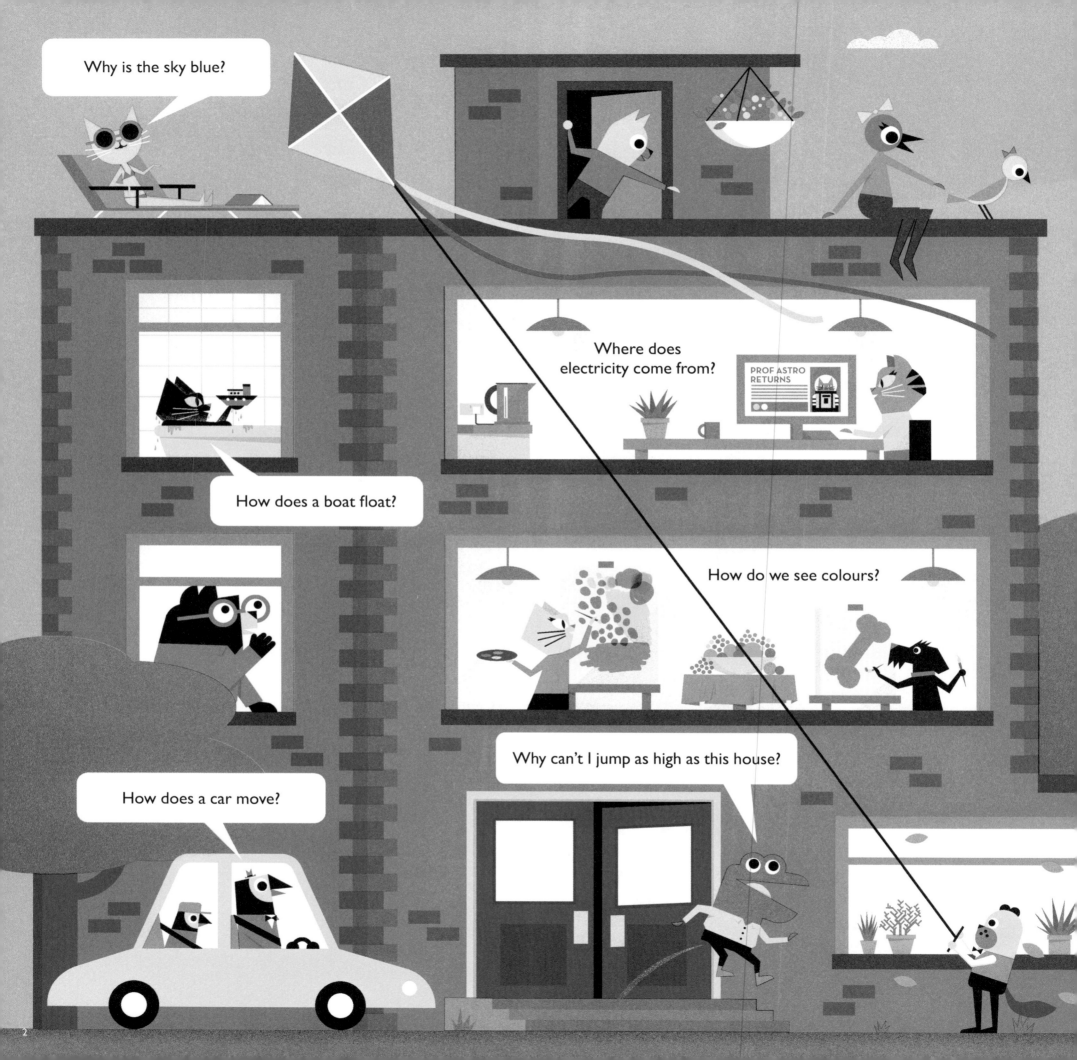

How do planes stay in the air?

How do birds know north from south?

Oh, hello there, friends! Did you know that **physics** is a very important part of our everyday lives?

Just go for a walk and you'll see for yourself. From the wind that rustles the trees and the Sun that keeps us warm, to the car that drives us around and the food that gives us energy to play, physics is all around us, all the time!

Follow me and we'll investigate the laws of the Universe, the fundamental rules that describe the nature of our world and beyond. So turn the page and join me, **Professor Astro Cat**, on my

ATOMIC ADVENTURE!

We can feel the wind, but why can't we see it?

Home, sweet, home!

GRAVITY

On Earth, there is a simple rule: what goes up, must come down. If I jump in the air or throw a ball really high, I know that the ball and I will always return back to the ground. This is because of **gravity**, which is an invisible force that pulls us down to the ground.

Gravity always pulls things together but never pushes things apart. If there was no gravity on Earth then we would all float around, which would make it difficult to eat and drink or see our friends.

GRAVITY KEEPS US ON THE GROUND

EVERYTHING IN ITS RIGHT PLACE

The more massive a thing is, the more force it exerts on us. We all stay on the surface of the Earth because it is the biggest thing that is nearest to us. The sun is so big that it exerts a huge force due to gravity.

This gravitational pull keeps our planets together so they don't fly off into outer space, and that is why the planets stay in orbit.

KEEPING OUR MOON IN THE SKY

Our Moon stays in orbit around the Earth because of the Earth's gravity. Our moon is always trying to fly away but the gravity of our Earth keeps it flying around us.

YAHOO!

ON THE MOON

JUMPING ON THE MOON

Gravity is smaller on the Moon because the Moon is smaller than the Earth. This means you are able to jump much higher there. You would still come back down to the ground but much slower than you would on Earth.

ON THE EARTH

WHO DISCOVERED GRAVITY?

We know about gravity because of very curious people called scientists that explore, test and think about how everything works around us. Isaac Newton was a scientist who discovered how gravity works – he realised that gravity was acting on everything, from an apple falling from a tree to the planets moving around the Sun. So before we begin our adventure, let's understand what a scientist does.

FOR GRAVITY'S SAKE

Gravity is the reason the Earth and the Sun were created from clouds of dust and gas floating around in space. Gravity started to pull them together until they collapsed in on themselves and as they fell inwards, they became increasingly compact and turned into the stars and planets we see around us today.

Science is the study of the world around us and scientists are people who look at the world and ask some very simple questions about it.

What is everything made of?

Why does everything move the way it does?

Why is everything arranged this way rather than any other way?

THE SCIENTIFIC METHOD

In order to answer these questions, scientists go out and investigate the world by performing **experiments**. An experiment is a test we carry out on something in the world to see if it will behave the way we think it will.

For example, we might like to find out where rainbows come from. Perhaps you've noticed that rainbows only seem to appear when there is sunshine and rain in the sky at the same time. So we might guess that some combination of sunshine and rain causes a rainbow. In scientific terms, this guess is called a **hypothesis**.

To see if our hypothesis is right or not, we can conduct an experiment! Let's try creating our own rain using a spray of water from a hosepipe, first spraying the water on a sunny day (where we expect to make a rainbow) and then spraying the water on a cloudy day (where we don't expect to make a rainbow).

HOW ABOUT TRYING THIS EXPERIMENT YOURSELF? WHAT DO YOU THINK WILL HAPPEN?

SUNNY DAY

CLOUDY DAY

When we do this experiment, we are collecting scientific **results**. If these results match our guesses, then our hypothesis is correct. If not, we will have to go back to the drawing board and try to work out what else might be causing the rainbows.

This is what scientists do all the time. They make a hypothesis about how the world works and then design an experiment to test it. When a hypothesis proves to be true, scientists explain why it is true using a theory.

MEASUREMENT

An important part of any experiment involves measuring and there are many ways that physicists can measure an experiment and many different instruments they can use to get accurate results.

The standard **measurement** that scientists use to measure lengths and distances everywhere in the world is the **metre**, which is about the width of a normal doorway.

1000 mm = 1 m
1000 m = 1 km

We use millimetres to measure very small things (there are a **thousand millimetres in one metre**) and kilometres to measure very large things (there are a **thousand metres in one kilometre**). To measure distance you can use a ruler or a metre stick.

CATEX

12
11 1
10 2
9 3
8 4
7 5
6

TICK
TOCK
TICK
TOCK

The standard unit of time is the second. There are **60 seconds in one minute** and **60 minutes in one hour**.

Clocks are a very important part of our everyday life because they show us when to get up and when to eat! But we also use time to measure how long it takes for something to happen. For example, how long do you think it will take you to run from one side of the playground to the other? You can measure how long this takes by using a stopwatch.

Temperature is used to measure how hot or cold something is. We use an instrument called the thermometer to measure temperature.

We measure temperature using units called Celsius or Fahrenheit. Zero degrees Celsius is the temperature at which pure water freezes (which is 32 degrees Fahrenheit). 100 degrees Celsius is the temperature at which pure water boils (which is 212 degrees Fahrenheit).

Scientists measure how much mass something has but this is not to be confused with measuring how much something weighs!

Weight is a measure of how heavy something is on the surface of the Earth when gravity is pulling it down. For example, an elephant has a large weight on Earth, but it would weigh virtually nothing out in space because there is almost no gravity pulling it down.

Mass is a measure of how much stuff, known as 'matter', there is inside something – and this stays the same wherever the thing is. So the elephant would have the same mass in space as it does on Earth, because it is still made out of the same stuff!

The standard unit of mass is the kilogram. One kilogram is the mass of a bag of sugar. Scientists use weighing scales to measure everyday masses, but they have much more complicated techniques to measure the lightest and heaviest things in our Universe.

WHAT IS EVERYTHING MADE OF?

The simplest question you can ask about the world is: what is everything made out of? Well, trees are made of wood, windows are made of glass and nuts and bolts are made of metal… but what are these materials made of?

Imagine cutting a block of cheese in half to make two smaller blocks of cheese, then picking one of the halves and cutting it in half again to make two even smaller pieces.

If you keep cutting the little bit of cheese over and over again, it will keep getting smaller and smaller. Do you think you could keep going forever? Or would you get to a tiny bit of cheese that you could no longer cut in two?

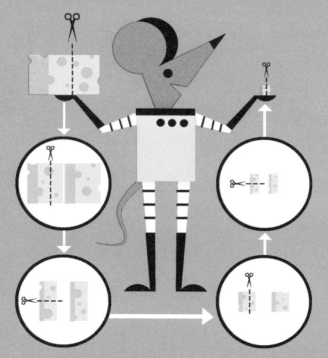

THE MAN BEHIND THE CHEESE

This cheese experiment comes from an ancient Greek philosopher called Democritus, who lived 2,400 years ago. He didn't have the tools to keep cutting the cheese smaller and smaller, so he did the experiment in his head. From this, he guessed that he would get down to a single unit that he called 'atomos'.

Atomos means 'indivisible' (something that cannot be divided or separated further) and is where the word 'atom' comes from. **Atoms** are amongst the smallest things that make up the world. It just goes to show that you can work out rather a lot just by thinking about things hard enough.

HOW SMALL IS AN ATOM?

We would need to use a super powerful microscope to see an atom because they are so incredibly tiny. If you were to sharpen a pencil so it was really sharp, how many atoms do you think there would be at the very tip of the pencil? Three atoms? Four atoms?

SLAM DUNK!

ATOMS AT THE TIP OF A PENCIL

To help put that into perspective, if all of the atoms in the pencil were the same type of atom and each atom was the size of a basketball, how big would the pencil be? Well, the pencil would reach all the way from the Earth to the Moon. It would be too gigantic for you or your parents to write with.

EARTH

Nope, there would be over ten trillion atoms right on that very tip of the pencil. That is **CRAZY SMALL**!

MOON

We're ready to activate, Professor Astro! 3, 2, 1..... GO!

To investigate further, I've built a 'scale invariant bubble transponder' so that Astro Mouse and I can show you what an atom looks like up close.

Psst! He means that he built a shrinking ray.

THE ATOM

Everything around us is made up of atoms, including you and me! You could say that atoms are the building blocks of the Universe. But what is an atom made of? Well, all atoms are made of the same three things: tiny particles called **protons**, **neutrons** and **electrons**.

These three particles are bundled together in different amounts to make the various types of atom. We usually think of protons, neutrons and electrons as little balls with different sizes.

A **proton** is a particle with a positive **charge**. This positive charge attracts electrons because electrons have a negative charge. Positive and negative charges are opposites that attract one another.

PROTON

ELECTRON

NEUTRON

A **neutron** is the same size as a proton but it has neither a positive nor negative charge, and that is why we call them neutrons – because they are neutral.

Protons and neutrons are found bundled together in the centre of the atom, which is called the **nucleus**, while the electrons are spread around the outside.

DIAGRAM OF AN ATOM

NUCLEUS

The lines in this diagram of an atom show the way that electrons move around the nucleus.

AN ATOM

ELECTRONS

Electrons are difficult to visualise, and we normally think of them as little balls whizzing around the nucleus at great speeds, similar to the planets orbiting around the Sun.

Our diagram isn't quite correct – in reality, electrons are spread out and fuzzy, covering the atom like a cloud. This is a more accurate view of what the laws of physics tell us!

If an atom was the same size as a football, the nucleus would be too small to see with human eyes.

A FOOTBALL

But if an atom was the size of a football stadium, you'd be able to see the nucleus deep in the centre. It would be difficult to find because it would be about the size of a pea.

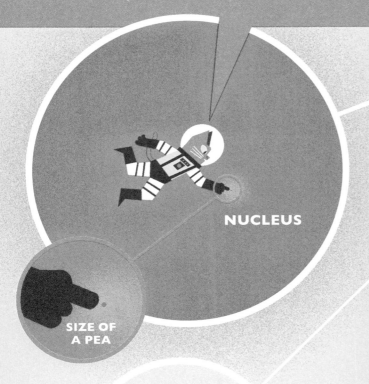

NUCLEUS

SIZE OF A PEA

FRUIT FLY

AN ATOM IS MAINLY MADE UP OF EMPTY SPACE

ELECTRONS WHIZZ AROUND THE NUCLEUS VERY FAST!

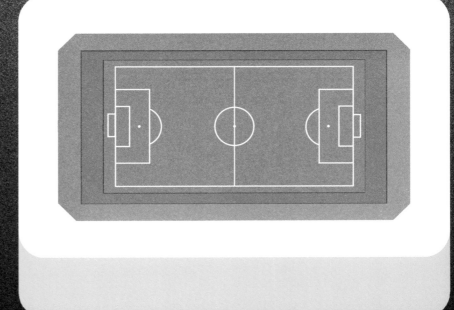

FOOTBALL STADIUM

If our nucleus was a pea the electrons would be like fruit flies whizzing around inside the stadium. As you can see, most of an atom is made up of empty space. That should make your brain tickle!

A WORLD OF ATOMS

HOW DO ATOMS BEHAVE?

Well, on Earth, at room temperature, atoms exist in 3 different forms which we call **SOLID, LIQUID AND GAS.**

Liquids are like water, they splash and flow and ripple. The atoms in liquids don't hold on to each other, but slide over and past each other.

THE WAY ATOMS ARE ARRANGED IN A SOLID

THE WAY ATOMS ARE ARRANGED IN A LIQUID

THE WAY ATOMS ARE ARRANGED IN A GAS

Solids are hard and don't really compress. If you look around you, most of what you see is a solid. All the atoms in a solid are locked together, holding on to each other really tight.

Gases, like the air around us, are thin and float about. The atoms in a gas are really far apart and only touch briefly when they bang into each other.

ELEMENTARY, MY DEAR ATOM!

There are many different types of solids, liquids and gases all around us. Some are light, some are heavy, some are hard and some are soft which means that there must be many different types of atoms too!

These different types of atoms are called **elements** and each element has a **different number of protons, neutrons and electrons** which gives them different abilities and appearances.

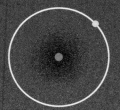

Hydrogen
is the lightest atom.
A hydrogen atom has
1 proton and 1 electron.

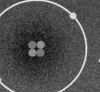

Helium
is the second lightest atom.
A helium atom has 2 protons,
2 neutrons and 2 electrons.

PERIODIC TABLE

Way back in 1869, **Dmitri Mendeleev** made a chart to organise all of the elements. He called it the **periodic table** and he arranged them in a special way starting with the element with the least amount of protons, Hydrogen, on the top left, to the element with the most protons, Ununoctium, on the bottom right.

The elements can be grouped into two main types: metals and non-metals.

 Metal

 Non-metal

 Metalloid

Unknown

The lightest elements are at the top of the periodic table and the heaviest are at the bottom.

1 H Hydrogen																		2 He Helium
3 Li Lithium	4 Be Beryllium											5 B Boron	6 C Carbon	7 N Nitrogen	8 O Oxygen	9 F Fluorine		10 Ne Neon
11 Na Sodium	12 Mg Magnesium											13 Al Aluminium	14 Si Silicon	15 P Phosphorus	16 S Sulphur	17 Cl Chlorine		18 Ar Argon
19 K Potassium	20 Ca Calcium	21 Sc Scandium	22 Ti Titanium	23 V Vanadium	24 Cr Chromium	25 Mn Manganese	26 Fe Iron	27 Co Cobalt	28 Ni Nickel	29 Cu Copper	30 Zn Zinc	31 Ga Gallium	32 Ge Germanium	33 As Arsenic	34 Se Selenium	35 Br Bromine		36 Kr Krypton
37 Rb Rubidium	38 Sr Strontium	39 Y Yttrium	40 Zr Zirconium	41 Nb Niobium	42 Mo Molybdenum	43 Tc Technetium	44 Ru Ruthenium	45 Rh Rhodium	46 Pd Palladium	47 Ag Silver	48 Cd Cadmium	49 In Indium	50 Sn Tin	51 Sb Antimony	52 Te Tellurium	53 I Iodine		54 Xe Xenon
55 Cs Caesium	56 Ba Barium	57-71	72 Hf Hafnium	73 Ta Tantalum	74 W Tungsten	75 Re Rhenium	76 Os Osmium	77 Ir Iridium	78 Pt Platinum	79 Au Gold	80 Hg Mercury	81 Tl Thallium	82 Pb Lead	83 Bi Bismuth	84 Po Polonium	85 At Astatine		86 Rn Radon
87 Fr Francium	88 Ra Radium	89-103	104 Rf Rutherfordium	105 Db Dubnium	106 Sg Seaborgium	107 Bh Bohrium	108 Hs Hassium	109 Mt Meitnerium	110 Ds Darmstadtium	111 Rg Roentgenium	112 Cn Copernicium	113 Nh Nihonium	114 Fl Flerovium	115 Mc Moscovium	116 Lv Livermorium	117 Ts Tennessine		118 Og Oganesson

More elements go in here

79 Au Gold

WHAT'S IN THE BOX?

The number in each box tells you how many protons there are in the nucleus of an atom, and this is called the atomic number.

The letters in the boxes are the chemical symbol for that element, which save us from having to write out the full name of the element.

Elements react with each other when they come into contact. Elements on the **left most column** are **very reactive** which means that they burn or explode really easily.

The elements on the **right most column** are generally **less reactive** which means they are more stable and safe.

ELECTRON

SHELLS

SHELLS

Each element has exactly the same number of electrons as protons in the nucleus.

Electrons live in layers which are called **shells** and each shell can hold a specific number of electrons before it is full.

On Earth, gold is very precious. A **gold atom** is quite heavy and has 79 protons, 118 neutrons and 79 electrons.

METALS AND NON-METALS

Most elements in the periodic table are **metals.** The main property of metals is that they **conduct electricity**, as their electrons are not tied to one atom but can hop from atom to atom freely.

A conductive metal allows its electrons to hop from atom to atom.

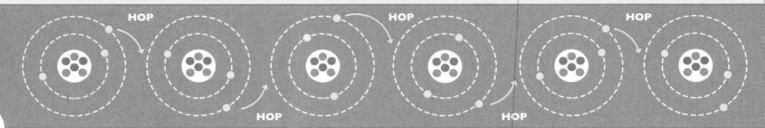

HOP HOP HOP

HOP HOP

Metals also **conduct heat** from one place to another very well and can be **bent into different shapes** when they are heated. Most metals are solid at room temperature.

BURP!

Vanadium is used to make strong tools that we use to fix things.

CRUNCH!

FIZZ

Aluminium is used for most drink cans and is light and soft so it is easy to crush.

Potassium is a very reactive metal and will explode if it touches water, so you wouldn't want to build a boat out of it!

Gold doesn't react with anything, which is why it can be used for false teeth and jewellery.

Iron is very strong and can support heavy weights. It is ideal for building houses and buildings.

Nickel is hard and easy to shape. It was once used to make coins.

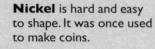

Copper is flexible and conducts electricity very well, which is why it is used for **electric wiring**.

ASTRO LABS
UNDER CONSTRUCTION

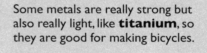

Some metals are really strong but also really light, like **titanium**, so they are good for making bicycles.

Unlike other metals, **Mercury** is liquid at room temperature.

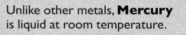

THERMOMETER

MERCURY

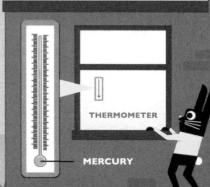

The other type of element in the periodic table are **non-metals.** Non-metals **don't conduct electricity or heat** very well and **most of them are actually gases** at room temperature.

Sulphur is yellow and brittle. It is used in gunpowder and in the heads of matches to light them.

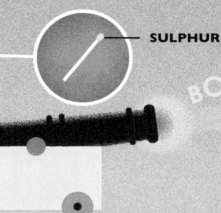

— SULPHUR

BOOM!

Oxygen is a non-metal and is very important on Earth because we need it to breathe.

ROOFTOP
YOGA

Helium is a noble gas, which is used in balloons and airships. This gas is very light and this helps things float.

CANNON CLUB ⬆
EVERY TUESDAY.

Neon is used in advertising signs on buildings. It glows orange when electricity passes through it. Neon lights are very popular in Las Vegas.

Diamonds 💎

P E N C I L
SHOP

Carbon is a solid non-metal element and can come in different forms such as a diamond, which is hard and see-through and used in wedding rings.

OPEN

Carbon is also used in graphite, which is soft and can be found in pencils to write with.

MOLECULES

If you imagine the letters in a word are atoms then a word is like a **molecule**. Most atoms don't like to be lonely so generally they don't travel around on their own.

Instead, **atoms join into groups with other atoms from many other elements to form molecules.** There are even more different types of molecule than there are different atoms.

MOLECULE

ASTRO

ATOM ATOM ATOM ATOM ATOM ATOM

A **compound** is a type of molecule just like an element is a type of atom. Pretty neat, huh?

MIXTURES

The air around us is made up of **Oxygen** and **Nitrogen** which are atoms that have come together to form molecules.

OXYGEN ATOM — OXYGEN MOLECULE — NITROGEN ATOM — NITROGEN MOLECULE

This is called a mixture because the Oxygen and Nitrogen **don't join together,** but are just **mixed up and can be separated.**

MOLECULES IN A MIXTURE

COMPOUNDS

Water is made of two different types of atoms: **one oxygen atom** and **two hydrogen atoms.** If a molecule is made up of two or more different types of atoms we call it a **compound.**

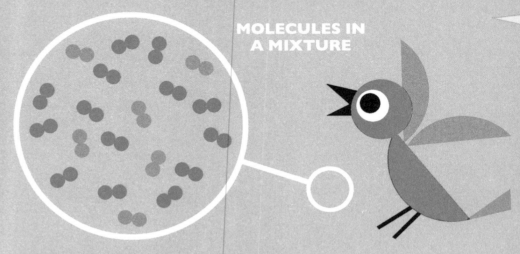

OXYGEN ATOM + HYDROGEN ATOMS = WATER MOLECULE

It is called a compound because **the atoms are chemically joined together so that they cannot be separated.**

Er... help, I'm stuck. I'm too young to be a compound!

REACTIONS

When certain chemical substances touch, they can have a **chemical reaction** where the atoms are rearranged to form new molecules with different properties. Different reactions can behave very differently from one another.

A firework is a **fast reaction** that happens when the powder in the firework reacts with the oxygen in the air. This kind of reaction doesn't happen on its own, it needs some heat to start it off which is why you light the fuse.

When iron goes **rusty,** it is because water and oxygen in the air reacts with the iron to create a new molecule called **iron oxide.** This is a **slow reaction** and takes years.

FFSSSSSSSSSSSSSSSSS

RUST

By joining together different elements in different ways, you can make new materials which combine the abilities of different elements. **Iron** is really strong, but snaps when pulled apart and rusts.

To make it stronger we can add **carbon,** which creates a compound called **steel.** Then we can add **chromium** to it to make **stainless steel** so it doesn't rust! Hooray!

CHANGES

Aloha, friends! As you know, when lots of atoms and molecules are all together in one place they can exist as solids, liquids and gases but if there is a change in their environment then they can change too.

Water is usually a liquid but we can turn it into a solid called ice by freezing it in a freezer. Ice makes our drinks lovely and cold!

WHAT IS AIR?

The air around us is a gas. It might look like there is nothing in the air, but it is actually full of many different atoms and molecules, all flying about and crashing into you. The air is made of a mixture of chemicals, but it is mostly made of nitrogen (78%) and oxygen (21%).

HOTTING UP!

If we **heat** up and boil water, it can turn into a **gas.** The bubbles in the boiling water are actually **water vapour,** which is water that has turned into a gas. This water vapour gas is the **steam** that comes from the top of a hot drink.

DID YOU KNOW?

At everyday tempaeratures air molecules travel on average over 1,000 miles per hour! Incredible!

Even when there is no wind and the air seems like it is standing still, it isn't! The molecules in the air are still zipping around really fast!

LIQUID WATER MOLECULES CHANGING INTO WATER VAPOUR

TOO HOT TO HANDLE!

It is not just water that can be a solid, a liquid or a gas. If you heat anything up enough, it will melt into a liquid and eventually boil off into a gas. We are used to rocks being solid, but inside a volcano the rock is so hot it turns into a liquid and flows out in the form of lava.

COOLING OFF

When a solid heats up it expands and gets bigger and when a solid cools down it contracts and gets smaller. Liquids and gases also expand with heat. As they heat up the atoms have more energy which makes them jiggle and bang into each other more vigorously.

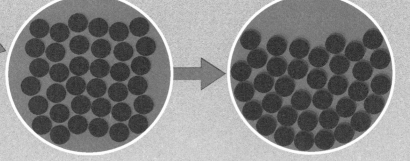

ATOMS IN A SOLID

ATOMS JIGGLE AND SPREAD OUT AS THEY GET HOTTER

ATOMS JIGGLE FASTER AND TURN INTO A LIQUID FORM

PRETTY AND PRECIOUS

Solids can come in different forms and **crystals** are particularly interesting. In a crystal, **the atoms or molecules that make it up are arranged in a repeating pattern over and over again.**

JIGGLE AND WIGGLE

The hotter the liquid is, the more the molecules jiggle about and the easier they move past each other. So lava straight out of the volcano flows really fast because it's so hot, but as it cools down it gets slower and slower, until finally it hardens into rock.

ALL ABOUT THE ANGLES

This makes crystals very pretty to look at because they form nice patterns – and they glitter because light reflects off their surfaces at different angles.

MASS AND DENSITY

Some things are big and heavy, like elephants, and other things are small and light, like butterflies. More interestingly, there are things that are big but also light, like hot air balloons, and other things that are small but heavy, like a block of lead. How can this be? Well, it can all be explained through the relationship between **mass** and **density**.

WHAT IS MASS?

Mass is a measurement of how much stuff is inside of something. Anything that is made of atoms has mass, and on Earth we can measure the mass of something by putting it on the weighing scales and seeing how many grams or kilograms it weighs.

WHAT IS DENSITY?

Some things are the same size but have different masses. Imagine having two toy footballs — one is made of foam, like the stuff a bath sponge is made of, and the other is made of stone.

Even though they are the same size, one is much heavier than the other. You might want to know which is which before you kick one or your foot will get a nasty surprise!

FOAM

STONE

INCREASE AND DECREASE

The reason the foam ball is lighter is because it has less mass in the same space, so its matter is more spread out. To put it another way, it is less dense. You can tell this is the case because it would be easy to squish it down into a much smaller ball. If you did this, there would still be the same amount of foam there – but because you crushed it down to a smaller size, you would have increased its density.

HOT AIR RISES AND IS CAUGHT BY THE BALLOON

Foam molecules when less dense.

Foam molecules when more dense.

TOPSY TURVY

In general, solid things are always more dense, which is why rocks are heavy. Liquid things are a bit less dense (although not always), while gases are the least dense. This is because gas atoms are spread really far apart. Less dense things float on top of more dense things, which is why the air floats above the ground and the sea. It would be really weird if it was the other way around!

HOW DOES A HOT AIR BALLOON STAY IN THE SKY?

Hot air balloons work by heating up air. Hot air expands and so is less dense than cold air. This means that it wants to go upwards to float on top of the cold air. But hot air balloons catch that hot air in a big bag and stop it from escaping, so the hot air ends up dragging the whole balloon up with it, basket and all!

FLOATING

Some things float on water while other things sink but this doesn't depend on how big they are. For example, an iceberg can be huge but it will still float on water but a small pebble will sink to the bottom. **How can this be?**

Well, ice is strange – it's a solid thing that floats on a liquid thing! **This means that ice is less dense than water.**

Helium is a good gas to blow up a balloon with. It floats because it is less dense than the air.

DO WE FLOAT?

Our bodies are a very similar density to water, which means we just about float on water. It is easier to float in salty seawater because salt water is denser than fresh water due to salt molecules.

A very salty sea, like the Dead Sea in the Middle East, would allow us to float very easily.

In liquid water, the molecules can move about next to each other in any old way but when water freezes into ice, it expands and gets bigger. All the water molecules join together in a way that makes them spread out a little bit.

WATER MOLECULES

WATER MOLECULES WHEN FROZEN

DIVE, DIVE, DIVE!

Submarines have special tanks that are filled with air or water. When a submarine floats on water, it means that its tanks are full of air.

The submarine carefully balances the amount of air and water in its tanks so that it counteracts the upward thrust of the ocean and can dive under water.

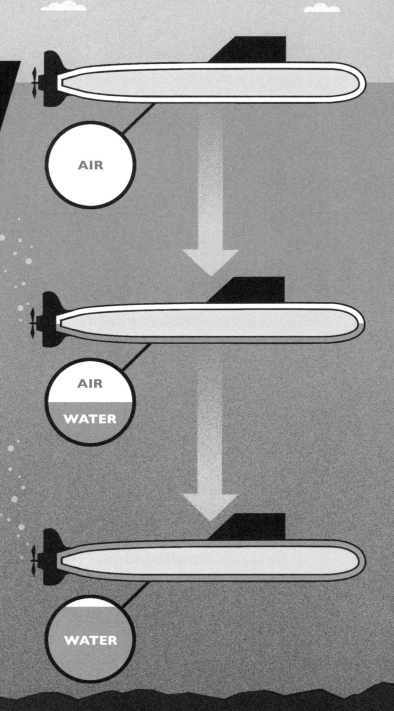

AYE AYE, CAPTAIN!

If huge ships are made of very heavy steel and iron, how does a ship float? Surely, it's impossible?

Ships are not solid metal all the way through or they would sink straight away. The outside of the ship is a steel and iron shell and the inside of a ship is mainly empty space containing lots of air.

Air is less dense than water so the ship's overall density is less than the water which means it can float. Pretty cool, huh, shipmates?

UPWARD THRUST

Everything in water experiences an **upward thrust** force. If an object's weight is smaller than its upthrust, it will float, but if its weight is greater than the upthrust it will sink. The size of the upthrust is equal to the weight of water that the object displaces.

So if this ship had a hole and filled up with water, it would gradually become more dense and sink. Quick, abandon ship!

It is this careful balance of water and air that stops the submarine sinking to the bottom of the ocean.

A WORLD IN MOTION

Cars drive along the roads, apples fall from trees and birds fly through the air. Many things around us move about and all of these follow the same rules of motion, which we can explain by using measurements.

DISTANCE
This is how far something moves.

TIME
This is how long the object is moving for.

SPEED
This is how fast the thing we are looking at is moving.

GO, GO, GO!

At the beginning of a race, a race car goes from standing still on the starting grid to travelling really fast in a very short amount of time. **Acceleration** is how much faster you get every second.

GO!

ACCELERATION

Things don't just travel around at the same speed all the time because sometimes they speed up or slow down. If something speeds up, we say it accelerates, and if something slows down, we say it **decelerates**.

MEASURING MOTION

In physics, we look at how many metres something moves each second **(m/s)** but people also use miles per hour **(mph)** or kilometres per hour **(kph)**.

RUNNING AT TOP SPEED
12 m/s
27 mph
43 kph

CYCLING
16 m/s
35 mph
57 kph

CHEETAH RUNNING
33 m/s
74 mph
119 kph

THE STEADY PASSENGER

If you don't look out of the window of a moving car, it seems like you are sitting perfectly still. This is because both you and the car are travelling at the same speed, so you stay together.

RACE CAR
104 m/s
233 mph
375 kph

ZOOMING AROUND THE SUN

Would you believe that you are travelling at an incredible speed even when sitting still on a nice comfy chair at home? **Both you and the chair are hurtling through space at colossal speeds as the Earth flies around the Sun.**

The Earth is travelling around the Sun at an amazing 107,000 kph or 66,700 mph! You don't feel like you are moving because the Earth moves at a fixed and steady speed, which carries us along **like passengers in a car** so it seems like everything is still.

FORCES

So how do things get moving? It's because of **forces**. If something is standing still, the only way it can start moving is either by it producing a force or having a force act upon it. If you are sitting on a swing, you need someone to give you a good push to start swinging — that's a type of force! And there are many different kinds.

Pushing and pulling forces are used when you want to move something from one place to another. Like when I have to push Astro Mouse out of his bed and pull him down to breakfast.

PUSH

PULL

DEFYING GRAVITY

For an aeroplane to lift off the ground it needs to produce a force that overcomes the force of gravity. It does this by creating a lift force with its wings. In part the plane does this because of its wing's shape.

Because of the wing's shape, air moves over the wing faster than the air moving under it. This makes the **air pressure** below the wing higher than the pressure above the wing, which creates a lift force.

Air molecules are more spread out because it is curved (less pressure).

WING   AIR

Air molecules are more tightly packed because it is straight (more pressure).

Things moving through the air also feel a **friction** force, which we call **air resistance**. The faster you go, the more air resistance there is, which is why fast cars and aeroplanes are shaped like wedges — they can cut through the air better and reduce the friction against them.

JET AEROPLANES EXPERIENCE ALL SORTS OF FORCES AS THEY ZOOM THROUGH THE SKY.

Twisting force to raise and lower the flaps on the wings and the rudder on the tail of the jet plane to control direction and elevation.

Drag force due to the friction of air resistance from air banging into the jet plane.

DRAG

JET ENGINE

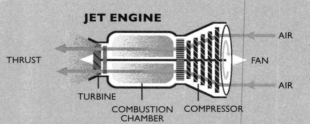

THRUST

AIR

FAN

AIR

TURBINE

COMBUSTION CHAMBER

COMPRESSOR

Turning force in the jet engine to turn the fan inside to push air out the back.

Cars produce turning forces in their wheels to make them roll forwards or backwards.

Are we there yet?

AIRFIELD

AIR UNICORN

AIR TIGER

A **turning** force is when something is twisted, like when you open a jam jar.

A **compression** force is when something is being squashed, like when you sit on a cushion.

HELP!

LIFT

Lift force produced by the wings.

THRUST

Thrust from the engine pushing the jet plane forwards.

DRAG

A parachute has lots of air resistance because it is so big, which creates a wide area for the air to push against. This is good because it stops you from falling too fast!

WEIGHT

Weight of the plane due to the force of gravity.

WEIGHT

A **spring** force is where something is being compressed or stretched and wants to return to its original shape. This happens in springs or the rubber bands on swimming goggles.

Levers are used to multiply forces. They turn a force at one end into a much bigger force at the other. This is how you can lift up a whole car using a car jack. The lever turns the force from your leg into a much bigger force in the jack – enough to lift the car!

The fulcrum is the fixed point of a lever that stays still while other parts move.

LOAD

EFFORT

x10

FULCRUM

A **tension** force is when something is being pulled apart, like the rope in a game of tug of war.

It's **MY** turn to wear the super cool jacket!

NO! It's **MY** turn!

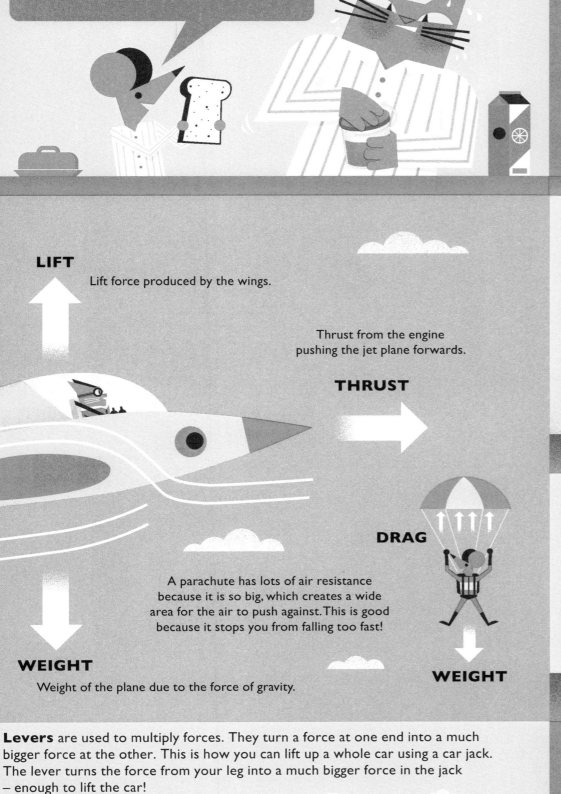

FORCES

When a force acts on an object, it makes it accelerate. You can see this when you drop a snowball and the force of gravity makes it accelerate towards the ground.

But some objects just stand still... Let's take the case of a skier standing still on a flat bit of mountain. What's happening? Where have the forces gone?

The force of gravity is still there, because everything on Earth always feels the force of gravity. But an equal force going in the opposite direction exactly cancels it out. This force comes from the ground and is called a reaction force. If something isn't moving, it means all of the forces acting on it are cancelling each other out.

THE FORCE OF GRAVITY FROM THE CUP

REACTION FORCE

GRAVITY PULLS US DOWN TO THE GROUND

REACTION FORCE CANCELLING OUT SKIER'S GRAVITY FORCE

NEED FOR SPEED

But what happens if the angle of the ground changes? Let's look at the start of the ski slope. Here the reaction force stops pointing directly upwards and starts pointing at a slight angle, so it no longer cancels out the force of gravity.

SKIER'S GRAVITATIONAL FORCE INTO THE GROUND

GRAVITATIONAL FORCE PULLING SKIER DOWN THE SLOPE

FASTER, FASTER!

There is a little bit of gravity left, which starts pulling the skier down the slope. The steeper the slope, the faster the skier goes!

REACTION FORCE IS NOW TILTED

PRESSURE

Remember how we talked about air pressure lifting planes? Well, **pressure** is really a measure of how spread out or focused a force is.

If you focus a force into a point, it has a lot more pressure than if the same force is spread out. This is why spiky shoes are good for walking on ice because they focus your weight into spikes that smash through the ice to help you grip. A normal shoe would slip on the icy surface when you tried to move, because the flat sole of the shoe doesn't exert enough pressure to grip.

Sometimes you want to spread forces out and create low pressure. An example of this is snowshoes, which spread your weight out over a large area by making your feet bigger. Because of the larger surface area, the pressure of your feet becomes smaller – now you can stand on top of the snow instead of sinking down into it!

FORCE IS FOCUSED INTO A POINT CREATING HIGH PRESSURE

THE FOCUS OF THE FORCE IS SPREAD OUT. THIS CREATES A LOWER PRESSURE.

DID YOU KNOW?

You might think that heavy things fall faster than light things, but this is not true. The acceleration from gravity is the same, no matter what your mass is. The reason things fall at different speeds is because of **air resistance** – on Earth, things with a large surface area tend to feel more air resistance than things with a small surface area.

The astronaut David Scott showed this when he was on the Moon, where there is no air and so no air resistance. He dropped a feather and a hammer at the same time… and they hit the ground at exactly the same time!

FEELING THE PRESSURE

Pressure is not just felt by solid things. Liquids and gases feel it too. The pumping of your heart creates pressure that moves blood around your body. Even the air around you puts pressure on your body but you don't really feel it because our bodies push back.

AIR PRESSURE

Air molecules are banging into us all the time but we can't feel each one because they are so amazingly small. All these little molecules bouncing off you combine together to create air pressure.

The more air molecules bounce off you every second, the higher the air pressure.

THE FORCE OF AIR PRESSURE IS FELT EVENLY ALL OVER YOUR BODY

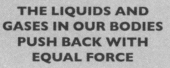

THE LIQUIDS AND GASES IN OUR BODIES PUSH BACK WITH EQUAL FORCE

Air pressure is caused by the weight of all the air in the atmosphere pushing down.

We get the highest air pressure at sea level and lower air pressure up a mountain because there is less air above you pushing down.

Changing air pressure is what makes your ears pop!

UNDER PRESSURE

The deeper you go underwater, the higher the pressure gets and it gets high really fast because water is so heavy.

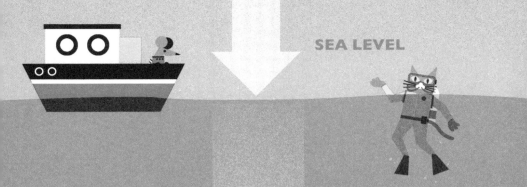

SEA LEVEL

Just diving **10 metres** underwater increases the pressure on your body by double the amount at sea level.

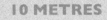

10 METRES

If you go down **20 metres** the pressure is three times the amount of atmosphere pressure than at sea level.

20 METRES

Because the pressure increase happens very quickly, scuba divers need to dive carefully in stages so their bodies can gradually adjust to the increase in pressure. They also need to be very careful when coming back to the surface because a dramatic change in pressure can make you very ill.

CRUNCH!

DEEP, DEEP DOWN

Deep sea divers have to wear special protective suits to protect them from the incredibly high pressure of the ocean's depths. The deeper they dive the more extreme the pressure is on their whole body.

They can go as far as 700 metres and the pressure is like a whole elephant standing on your foot but spread across your whole body. If they took off the suit, the water would squash them like a grape.

NEWTON'S LAWS

My friend, **Isaac Newton**, first explained the rules of forces and movement in 1687 by conducting his own experiments. Using what he discovered, he created **three** famous laws of nature called **Newton's Laws.**

FIRST LAW

An object which isn't moving won't start moving unless a force is applied to it. Things that are already moving will keep on moving in the same direction at the same speed until something stops them.

ISAAC NEWTON

THE FORCE OF FRICTION

Most things that are moving tend to slow down and stop because they feel the force of friction from whatever they are moving over. **If there was no friction, things would keep moving in the same direction at the same speed forever!**

ON THE SURFACE

Different surfaces have different amounts of friction. It is easier to go sledging down a snowy hill in winter than a grassy hill in summer because the **snow has less friction than the grass.**

SLIP AND SLIDE

Less friction makes things really **slippery**, like trying to walk on ice. A large amount of friction makes it really hard to move, like wading through water.

Friction can be a hindrance but also a help. If there was no friction when we tried to walk, our feet would just slip back and forth and we'd never get anywhere!

SECOND LAW

When you push something with lots of mass it doesn't speed up as much as something with less mass.

Think of pushing a go-cart – if it's empty, it will be **light** and easy for you to push. But if it's got a big bear in it, it will be **heavy** and much harder to push.

YAHOOOOOOOO!

FASTER, PROFESSOR!

ACCELERATING

Newton has an equation to back this up: **force = mass × acceleration** (or $F = ma$).

If one go-cart has twice the mass of the other, and you push them both with the same force, the lighter go-cart will accelerate twice as much as the heavier go-cart.

THIRD LAW

When one object puts a force on a second object, the second object pushes back with the same force.

RECOIL

When a cannon shoots a cannonball, it fires it out with a lot of force. But the cannonball also pushes back on the cannon, creating a big spring back called **recoil.**

RECOIL

BOOM!

CANNONBALL

This is why **cannons are made to be much bigger and heavier than the cannonballs,** because the more mass a cannon has, the smaller the recoil is.

ENERGY

Energy makes everything around us happen! Whenever anything changes in any way it is because energy is being turned from one form into another. **It can never be created or destroyed, only transformed.** So the Universe contains exactly the same amount of energy today as it did when it first began!

LIGHT ENERGY

Light is also a form of energy and this is how we are able to see things. Little waves of light give up their energy to our eyes, which then send a signal to our brains and this allows me to spot when a crime is being committed!

HELP!

POW!

KINETIC ENERGY

Anything that moves around has a type of energy called **kinetic energy**. I use kinetic energy when I judo chop super villains.

POTENTIAL ENERGY

If you lift something off the ground, you are giving it **potential energy** because it has the 'potential' to be released as soon as you let go. Just like when I lift this bomb and prepare to throw it somewhere safe!

HEAT ENERGY

Anything that is warm contains **heat energy** and the explosion from this bomb gives off a lot of heat. The hotter something is, the more heat energy it contains.

CHEMICAL ENERGY

Eating food is great! Not only does it taste good but it's also full of **chemical energy**. We absorb this energy for ourselves using our stomachs, which extract it by digestion. We can then use this energy to power our bodies!

BURNING UP!

Whenever we burn something, we also use up its chemical energy. Wood has chemical energy stored inside it. When we burn it, the chemical energy is turned into heat and light energy.

FROM ONE TO THE OTHER!

When energy gets converted from one type to another, exactly the same amount has to come out as goes in.

For example, let's look at the **Astro Mobile**: it uses **petrol** because it has lots of chemical energy stored inside it; when it is burned by a car engine, most of the energy goes into making the wheels move.

PETROL PUMP

WASTE NOT, WANT NOT

But not all of it – a lot turns into heat and sound. This heat and sound energy isn't very useful, as it doesn't make the car move. What a waste! When we build machines, we want them to waste as little energy as possible. **The better a machine is at not wasting energy, the more efficient it is.**

ENERGY AND POWER

On Earth, we get almost all of our energy from the Sun. The Sun releases huge amounts of energy every second in the form of light and heat, and over millions of years this energy has been absorbed on Earth and turned into plants and animals.

To supply us with plenty of energy to make things work, we have built **power stations.** There are many different types of power stations that all **generate energy in very different ways.**

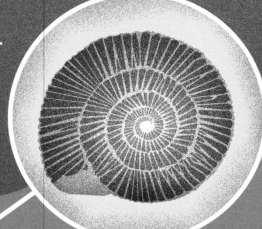

FOSSIL

COUGH COUGH

POWER STATIONS

Most power stations burn **fossil fuels,** like coal or natural gases that are found in the Earth. They burn these fuels to create heat energy, which is then changed into electrical energy to power our homes and schools. We call them fossil fuels because they are made up of dead plants or dead sea creatures.

Unfortunately, these power stations also release pollution into the atmosphere when they burn fuel, which is bad for wildlife, the environment and us.

NUCLEAR POWER

Nuclear power stations get their energy from splitting very heavy atoms apart, like uranium. Uranium is the largest natural element that we can mine on Earth, so it can be split down into other lighter elements which releases huge amounts of energy at the same time.

Unfortunately, nuclear power stations can produce radioactive waste which is very dangerous.

URANIUM ATOM

RENEWABLE ENERGY

Some power stations don't need any fuel but instead make energy from the blowing of the wind or running water in a river. We call this **renewable energy**.

SOLAR POWER

Energy can also be collected directly from the Sun using **solar panels**. These use special materials which produce electricity when sunlight shines on them.

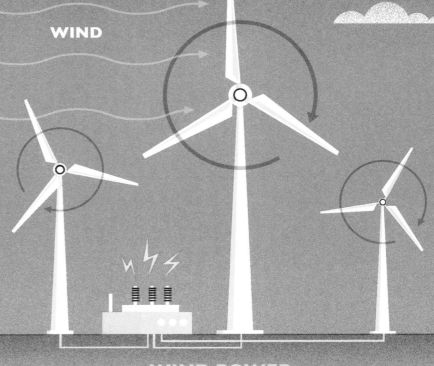

WIND

WIND POWER

Wind turbines use the energy of the wind to spin a big propeller. This turning motion is converted into electricity.

WATER POWER

We can also generate electricity from waterfalls. When water runs from the top of a mountain all the way to the sea, it loses a lot of **potential energy.**

We can capture this potential energy by building a **hydroelectric dam**. Water rushing through one of these dams turns big wheels, which then generate electricity.

RESERVOIR

HYDROELECTRIC DAM

INTAKE

GENERATOR

TURBINE

POWERLINES

RIVER

ELECTRICITY

Electricity is a very useful form of energy because it can be easily changed into other forms of energy, like heat and light. We use electricity every day and it is what keeps our **light bulbs, TVs and computers on.** Electricity comes from the movement of electrons.

Some materials contain electrons that are free to hop from one atom to another and this type of material is called an **electrical conductor.** The best conductors of electricity are metals like **copper** or **gold.**

INSULATION

Anything that doesn't have free moving electrons cannot conduct electricity and is called an **insulator.** Most of the materials around us are insulators, like **wood** and **plastic.**

ELECTRONS

SHELLS

TRANSPORTING ELECTRONS

Electrons move about in metal wires when they are connected to a source of energy like a battery or a power station. This is how our homes get electricity. They are connected to a big grid of electrical wires which have power stations at the other end.

The power stations create electricity which is moved through wires and into our homes.

We can measure the amount of electrons moving through a conductor and we call this **electrical current.** The more electrons that flow the higher the current.

VOLTAGE

Voltage is a measure of how much energy each electron has. The strength of batteries is measured in voltage and the higher the voltage the more electrical energy the battery produces.

WHEN LIGHTNING STRIKES

Lightning is a sudden release of electrical energy bursting through the sky at incredible speeds during a thunderstorm. This happens when particles inside the cloud become electrically charged as air and water molecules rub against each other.

The build up of electrons at the bottom of the cloud gets so big that it forces the air to turn from an insulator into a conductor, and in a split second a huge amount of electrons is released in a flash of lightning.

CREATE STATIC ELECTRICITY BY RUBBING A BALLOON UP AND DOWN ON YOUR JUMPER

STATIC

Static electricity is a build up of electrons that can be formed in some materials by rubbing them together. If you rub a balloon on your jumper, the balloon will lose electrons to your jumper. The balloon now has more positively charged protons than electrons, so it is positively charged. Now if you put the balloon against the wall, the static will make the balloon stick to the wall as if by magic.

ELECTRICITY IS DANGEROUS TO TOUCH

Lightning strikes tall things! Skyscrapers and tall buildings have electrical rods in the top of them to conduct the electricity safely into the ground so no one gets hurt.

MAGNETISM

Magnetism is how we can tell north from south on Earth. But what is it and where does it come from? It comes from magnets which are amazing! They are little blocks that can push and pull each other with invisible force fields called a **magnetic field**.

OPPOSITES ATTRACT

The rule that 'opposites attract' applies to magnets – if you try to push the north poles of two magnets together, they will repel each other, and the same thing will happen with the south poles.

| S | N | N | S |

| S | N | S | N |

BUT IF YOU PUT A NORTH AND A SOUTH POLE TOGETHER, THEY'LL ATTRACT AND STICK TOGETHER.

A REALLY BIG MAGNET

In fact, **the Earth is a giant magnet** with a north and south pole and a magnetic field that covers the entire surface of the Earth. This is extremely useful because it lets us use a compass to work out directions.

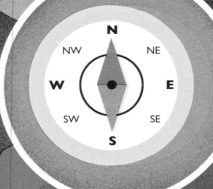

THE COMPASS

The needle in a compass is itself a little magnet, which lines up with the Earth's magnetic field, showing us north, south, east and west.

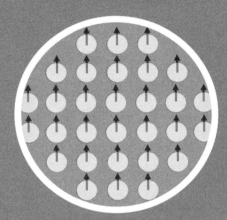

Follow me!

Animals like birds use the Earth's magnetic field to sense when they are travelling north or south as they migrate to look for warm places in the winter and cool places in the summer.

MAGNETIC ATOMS

Magnetism comes from how atoms line up in a material. Each atom is a tiny little magnet. If they all line up together, all the tiny little magnetic fields add together and create a big magnetic field.

In non-magnetic materials the atoms point in random directions and so their magnetic fields cancel out and end up with no magnetic field.

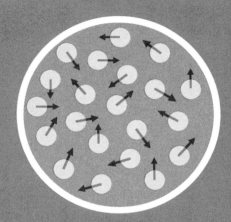

ATOMS IN A NON-MAGNETIC MATERIAL

ATOMS IN A MAGNETIC MATERIAL

MAKE YOUR OWN MAGNET

You can make your own magnet by making the atoms all line up in a metal. You can only do this with certain metals like iron and nickel where the atoms are able to rotate: this kind of metal is called **ferromagnetic.**

MAGNETIC PAPERCLIP

NON-MAGNETIC PAPERCLIP

S   N

1. Get a paperclip and a magnet and drag the paperclip over the magnet 100 times really fast in the same direction.

2. After you have done this your paperclip should also be magnetic and you can pick up other paperclips or staples. INCREDIBLE!

43

SOUND WAVES

Sounds are produced when things vibrate! **A vibration is a back and forth movement that happens very quickly.**

Let's look at my guitar! When I hit the strings, they vibrate and hit the air molecules next to them so that they vibrate too. **This vibration spreads out in a continuous wave through the air until it makes our ear drum vibrate making us hear the sound.**

AIR MOLECULES PUSH INTO ONE ANOTHER

This vibration of air molecules acts like a wave which we call a **sound wave.** When you drop a pebble into a lake, you create waves that ripple outwards. Sound waves are similar as they **make the air wobble in all directions from the sound source.**

MEDIUM

Most waves need a material to travel through. We call this material a medium. So, **water waves travel through the medium of water** and **sound waves travel through the medium of air.**

PUMP UP THE VOLUME

If a sound is very loud then it has big vibrations but very quiet sounds have little vibrations.

We use the word volume to describe how big or small a sound is.

A ROCKET BLASTING OFF CREATES A VERY LOUD SOUND.

A WHISPER TO A FRIEND CREATES A VERY QUIET SOUND.

RUMBLING IN THE SKY

You may have noticed that during a thunderstorm you always see the lightning before you hear the rumble of thunder. This is because **light travels faster than sound through the air**. You can use the time between seeing lightning and hearing thunder to measure how far away a storm is.

When you see lightning, just count the seconds until you hear thunder – **for every 3 seconds you count, the lightning is almost 1 kilometre away.**

A BAT'S HIGH PITCH SQUEAK BOUNCES OFF A BUTTERFLY SO THAT IT KNOWS WHERE IT IS IN THE DARK

ECHO ECHO ECHO

When you hear an echo it is because the sound waves of your voice have bounced off something and come back to you. This is called **reflection**.

Bats use the reflection of their squeaks to hear what is around them. They use their ears as eyes because they like living in dark places, like a cave.

PITCH PERFECT

How frequently a vibration wobbles back and forth in a second is called a **frequency**.

If a sound vibrates really **fast** then it has a high frequency and a **high pitch** and if the vibration is **slow** it has a low frequency and **low pitch**.

A BIRD SINGS IN A HIGH PITCH

A TIGER'S ROAR IS IN A LOW PITCH

LIGHT AND COLOUR

Light is the fastest thing in the Universe. **It can travel around the Earth seven and half times in one second!**

Light is how we see the world around us and why different things are different colours. When we see the things around us in the daytime, we are seeing the light that comes from the Sun bouncing off whatever we are looking at!

WHITE LIGHT FROM THE SUN CONTAINS ALL THE COLOURS MIXED UP

LEAVES ABSORB ALL THE WHITE LIGHT EXCEPT GREEN

So how come there are so many different colours around us when the light from the Sun appears to be just one colour?
Well, even though light from the Sun is white, white light actually contains all the colours of the rainbow.

OUR EYES SENSE LIGHT AND COLLECT IT

GREEN LIGHT REFLECTED INTO OUR EYES

What makes something one colour rather than another?

This is all to do with how the light bounces off an object. Some colours are **absorbed** in the surface of the object, while other colours are reflected back out.

A green leaf looks green because it **reflects the green part of the white light back to you,** while it absorbs all the other colours.

SHADY SHADOWS

We cast a shadow because light shines in straight lines and cannot bend around objects unless they are see through, like a window, or are reflective, like a mirror.

OBJECTS CAST SHADOWS BECAUSE LIGHT CANNOT BEND AROUND THEM

LIGHT CAN PASS THROUGH A GLASS WINDOW BECAUSE IT IS SEE THROUGH

LIGHT WILL BOUNCE OFF A MIRROR BECAUSE IT IS REFLECTIVE

REMEMBER!

Never look directly at the Sun because it is so bright that it can damage your eyes. On a sunny day it is a good idea to wear sunglasses to protect your eyes but even then you still shouldn't look directly at the Sun.

BENDING THE LIGHT FANTASTIC

You can split white light into all the different colours by shining it through a triangular piece of glass called a prism.

Each colour bends a different amount — at one end is red, which gets bent the least, and at the other end is purple, which gets bent the most. Bending light is called refraction.

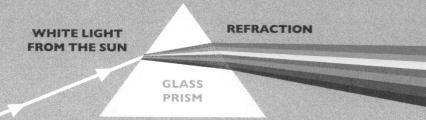

WHITE LIGHT FROM THE SUN

REFRACTION

GLASS PRISM

IN RAINBOWS

Rainbows appear due to **refraction** but it is a **raindrop that splits white light into different colours.** The light reflects, bouncing off the back of the raindrop and spreading out as it comes out of the raindrop. **When we see the light coming from all of the raindrops at once, we see a rainbow!**

The best way to see a rainbow is if the Sun is behind you and the rain is in front of you. The light flies over your head, bounces off the rain and comes back into your eyes.

WHITE LIGHT FROM THE SUN

RAIN DROP

WHITE LIGHT IS SPLIT INTO DIFFERENT COLOURS AND REFLECTED BACK AT OUR EYES

THE SCIENCE OF LIGHT

WHY IS THE SKY BLUE?

The sky behaves in the opposite way to most objects. Earth's atmosphere lets all of the light through apart from the blue light, which it scatters in every direction and because blue light goes in all directions, the whole sky looks blue no matter which way you look at it.

WHITE LIGHT FROM THE SUN CONTAINS ALL THE COLOURS MIXED UP

EARTH

SUN

AIR MOLECULES IN OUR ATMOSPHERE ABSORB SOME OF THE BLUE LIGHT AND SCATTERS IT ACROSS OUR SKY

THE ART OF SEEING

The colours of paints work differently to the colours from a light source like the Sun or a computer screen. **When you add all of the different colours of sunlight together you get white light but when you mix all the colours of paint together, you get a dark muddy brown!**

PRIMARY COLOURS OF LIGHT

PRIMARY COLOURS OF PAINT

BLACK ABSORBS ALL THE COLOURS

BLACK PAINT

WHITE REFLECTS ALL THE COLOURS

WHITE SURFACE

Each colour of paint only reflects one colour and absorbs all the other colours. So if you mix together lots of different colours of paint, you are left with a new colour that absorbs all of the colours so it looks closer to black.

With paint, black is all of the colours combined. With light, black is the absence of light. This is why it is difficult to say for certain if black and white are considered colours.

THE ELECTROMAGNETIC SPECTRUM

Light is an **electromagnetic wave**, and is just one of a whole range of different electromagnetic waves, all of which have different wavelengths — some waves are bigger than others.

Scientists organise the biggest to the smallest wavelengths on a scale called the **electromagnetic spectrum**. Here are some of the waves that the electromagnetic spectrum contains:

Radio Waves	Microwaves	Infrared	Visible Light	Ultraviolet	X-rays	Gamma rays

Radio waves are used for radio and TV signals. They have the biggest wavelengths.

Infrared (also known as heat) is given off by hot things, like our own bodies or a fireplace.

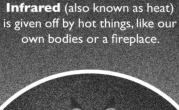

Microwaves are used to heat up food or to transmit our mobile phone signal.

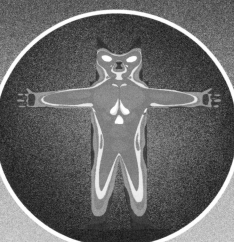

Visible light lets us see the world around us.

X-rays go right through you and bounce off your bones, so they're useful for scanning inside your body in a hospital.

Ultraviolet comes from the Sun and can hurt our skin — it's why we wear suncream!

Gamma rays have the highest energy and the smallest wavelengths. They are used in hospitals to help kill cancers, but they can also be dangerous to humans and other life. We use a radiation symbol to warn others if something is radioactive and dangerous.

AMAZING MATERIALS

Different collections of different atoms have different abilities. By combining atoms in all sorts of different ways, we can make materials that have never existed before and can do things we never thought possible!

WATER REPELLENT CLOTHES

I hate getting my clothes wet in the rain and I bet you do too! Don't worry because scientists have made amazing materials called **nanomaterials** that have lots of special properties, and one use is to make a special raincoat.

NANO NANO

'Nano' means super small and these incredible materials have tiny bumps in the surface just a few atoms deep. **These bumps make the water molecules stick together into droplets on the surface and roll away rather than soak in.**

This is called a hydrophobic layer because hydro means water and phobic means it is scared away! Yikes.

WATER DROPLETS

WATER DROPLETS

NORMAL MATERIAL

NANOMATERIAL

CLIMBING UP THE WALLS

Geckos are clever animals that can stick to just about anything, even the ceiling! If you zoom in on their toes, you'll see that they are made of loads of ridges of skin.

GECKO

CLOSE UP OF RIDGES IN A GECKO'S FOOT

Scientists are trying to use the ridges similar to **gecko feet** to make gloves and shoes that would let you climb up any wall or even walk across the ceiling!

CLOAK OF INVISIBILITY

One day, scientists hope to be able to make a person completely invisible! See through materials, like water or glass, naturally bend light in different ways, but scientists are trying to make special materials called **metamaterials** that can bend light in strange ways not found in nature.

HALTING LIGHT!

The speed of light is the fastest speed that anything can travel in the Universe but light only travels this fast in a vacuum, like outer space where there is no air.

Light slows down when it travels through objects, like water. Physicists have managed to slow light down so much that it stops and stands still in a medium called **rubidium gas!**

VISIONARY

Scientists have been playing around with bending light for hundreds of years using lenses and mirrors. This has allowed us to make microscopes to see into the smallest worlds and telescopes to see distant galaxies.

Normal lenses have limits – if you look too close or too far everything becomes blurry but not with **metamaterials!**

Scientists are trying to use these amazing materials to make perfect lenses that **never go blurry,** allowing you to see to infinity!

NUCLEAR PHYSICS

Most of the atoms around us are very stable and have stayed the same for billions of years but sometimes they join together or split apart.

NUCLEUS
MADE OF PROTONS
AND NEUTRONS

ATOM

The study of atoms splitting apart or joining together is called nuclear physics, named after the atomic nucleus found at the centre of an atom.

NUCLEAR FUSION

When atoms meet, they usually bounce off each other harmlessly. In extreme conditions, **atoms can smash into each other so hard that they join together** and form a new atom. We call this **nuclear fusion.**

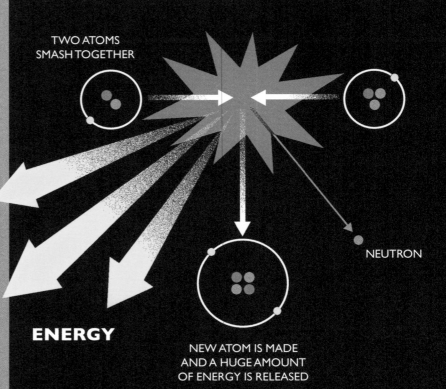

TWO ATOMS
SMASH TOGETHER

NEUTRON

ENERGY

NEW ATOM IS MADE
AND A HUGE AMOUNT
OF ENERGY IS RELEASED

When atoms fuse together, they release loads of energy in the form of heat, light and exotic particles. This same process is what powers the Sun!

HOT STUFF!

Scientists are trying to do this on Earth by building **nuclear fusion reactors,** which would provide us with huge amounts of clean energy to use. This is a very difficult task as it means recreating the scorching environment at the centre of the Sun here on Earth!

NUCLEAR FISSION

Some atoms are unstable because they have either too many or too few neutrons in their nucleus. **If this happens the atom will split apart into two smaller atoms which releases energy and new neutrons.** This is called **nuclear fission.**

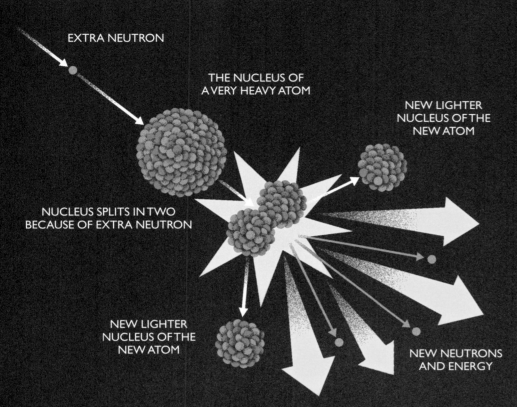

EXTRA NEUTRON

THE NUCLEUS OF A VERY HEAVY ATOM

NEW LIGHTER NUCLEUS OF THE NEW ATOM

NUCLEUS SPLITS IN TWO BECAUSE OF EXTRA NEUTRON

NEW LIGHTER NUCLEUS OF THE NEW ATOM

NEW NEUTRONS AND ENERGY

When atoms split apart, they release lots of energy, neutrons, and other subatomic particles which are called decay products.

$E = mc^2$

Albert Einstein's famous statement, $E = mc^2$, helps explain the amount of energy released in nuclear fusion or nuclear fission. **'E'** is energy, **'m'** is mass and **'c'** is the speed of light. The little 2 means you have to times everything by the speed of light twice.

$E = Mc^2$

The speed of light is so incredibly fast and such a huge number that this equation means that **a small bit of mass can turn into a humongous amount of energy!**

THE BLAST FROM AN ATOMIC BOMB LOOKS A BIT LIKE A MUSHROOM!

OH DEAR!

WEAPONS OF MASS DESTRUCTION

Nuclear fission and fusion was used in the creation of the first **atomic bomb.** This weapon is enormously destructive and was first used during World War 2 to devastating effect. The leftovers from nuclear bombs and from nuclear power are radioactive and are very dangerous to humans.

PARTICLE PHYSICS

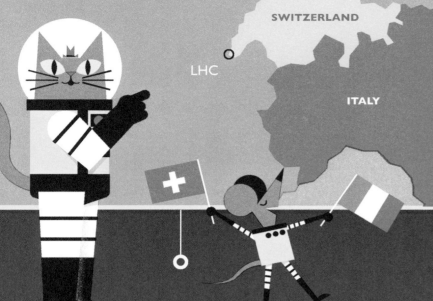

GERMANY

FRANCE

AUSTRIA

SWITZERLAND

LHC

ITALY

Scientists have spent a long time trying to find out what everything is made of. They found that if you split molecules apart, you get atoms. And if you split atoms apart, you get **subatomic particles** called protons, neutrons and electrons. **But what happens if you split these particles apart?**

LARGE HADRON COLLIDER

To find out, scientists built experiments like the **huge circular tunnel underground beneath the French-Swiss border** called the Large Hadron Collider.

This tunnel was built to shoot subatomic particles around in different directions.

Scientists wanted to see if they would split apart when they hit each other.

PARTICLE FEVER

This experiment revealed some strange **new subatomic particles**, all with different properties. As far as we know, the particles they discovered are the smallest things in the Universe!

ELECTRON

ATOM

QUARK QUARK

They found out that electrons can't be split into anything smaller but protons and neutrons can both be split into smaller particles called **quarks.**

NUCLEUS

SOLID

MOLECULE

QUARK!

PROTON

QUARK

QUANTUM PHYSICS

Quantum physics describes the laws of nature for the smallest things in our Universe. These are the rules that physicists see in nuclear and particle physics. In this tiny nanoscopic world, particles do seemingly impossible things and behave very strangely indeed!

LONG DISTANCE RELATIONSHIPS

Particles can talk to each other through a special quantum link even if they are separated by millions of miles.

This is called **entanglement.**

EXPECT THE UNEXPECTED

In our world, if you throw a ball against a wall it will bounce back at you, but in the quantum realm, if you throw a ball at a wall it might go straight through it!

This is called **quantum tunnelling.**

HAVE IT BOTH WAYS!

Can you spin around one way and spin around the other way at the same time? This is impossible for us to do but it's exactly what quantum particles do all the time.

Doing many opposite things at the same time is called **superposition.**

Although scientists understand a lot, we have no idea why the Universe behaves like this. So until we do, we just have to accept that the Universe is a rather strange place!

A STRANGE UNIVERSE

All of our knowledge about physics only describes a tiny 5% of the Universe. Through clever experiments scientists have found out that there is a huge amount out there that we simply don't understand.

PLANETS

STARS

ATOMS AND PARTICLES

DARK MATTER HELPS TO FORM GALAXIES

ORDINARY MATTER

5%

68%

DARK ENERGY

A DARK UNIVERSE

We understand that 'ordinary matter' is made up of atoms but scientists believe that **27%** of the Universe is made of a mystifying '**dark matter.**'

It is not like a planet or stars or a black hole. Dark matter is an invisible mass that does not create light, reflect light or absorb it.

27%

DARK ENERGY

The remaining **68%** of the Universe is made of mysterious dark energy, which we know almost nothing about and we have no idea where it comes from!

This strange force is making galaxies in the Universe accelerate away from each other, almost like a bizarre form of anti-gravity, which pushes outwards rather than pulling together.

WHAT DOES DARK MATTER DO?

Dark matter makes up **extra invisible mass inside galaxies** which makes them spin faster than if they were just made of normal matter.

It is believed that dark matter collects with other matter to help form galaxies, stars and planets. **If it wasn't for dark matter, we might not exist!**

THE MULTIVERSE

Some scientists think that there might be an infinite number of other Universes – a multiverse – some with slightly different laws of physics and others which are exactly the same as this one.

Each one of these would have **another version of you** in it, although unfortunately we don't yet know how to test this theory let alone travel there!

DECISIONS, DECISIONS!

One way of looking at quantum physics is to see many **different realities** where all different possibilities are acted out. So if you ever make a bad decision, take comfort in the fact that perhaps another you in another reality did the opposite!

LANGUAGE OF NUMBERS

Everything in this book has been described using words, but there is another language we use to talk about science: **mathematics.**

Much of the mathematics in science is captured in formulas. **Formulas** are combinations of symbols showing how things are related.

$$a^2 + b^2 = c^2$$

$$H_2O$$

$$E = m \times c^2$$

energy
mass
Speed of Light

If this is maths, then where are the numbers?
In formulas, we use letters in the place of numbers —

'd' for distance, **'s'** for speed, **'t'** for time.

So if you want to work out how far something moves (**d**), you take its speed (**s**) and multiply it by the time it takes (**t**).

$$d = s \times t$$

distance = speed × time

Let's see how far a snail can travel in 10 seconds compared to a race car.

As long as you know the speed of each thing, you can put the different numbers into the formula and find out the answer!

Speed of a snail = 0.013 metres per second, so d = 0.013m/s × 10s = 0.13 metres or 13 centimetres.

Speed of a race car = 90 metres per second, so d = 90m/s × 10s = 900 metres (nearly a kilometre).

The brilliant thing about formulas is that they apply to everything. So the formula above can be used for anything that moves around!

There are formulas for everything in physics, from the movement of stars to the wiggling of atoms.

THE NATURE OF MATHS

There is a deep connection between the nature of the Universe and mathematics. One example of this is the **Fibonacci series**, named after an Italian mathematician. Here's how to work out this series of numbers for yourself:

FIBONACCI SERIES

Start with 1 and 2. Add these together to get 3. Then add the last two numbers, 2 and 3, together to get 5. Just keep adding the last two numbers to get more and more numbers out:

3 + 5 = 8, 5 + 8 = 13, 8 + 13 = 21, 13 + 21 = 34 and so on.

The amazing thing about these numbers is they appear everywhere in nature from pinecones to trees.

If you count the petals on a flower, it will probably be one of these numbers.

LUCKY CLOVER

A clover has 3 leaves and four-leaf clovers are considered to be lucky because they are so rare and break the sequence in the Fibonacci series.

Mathematics doesn't stop there!
There's a huge range of things you can do with numbers and patterns. So next time you're doing your sums in maths class, remember that this is just the beginning of a fascinating journey!

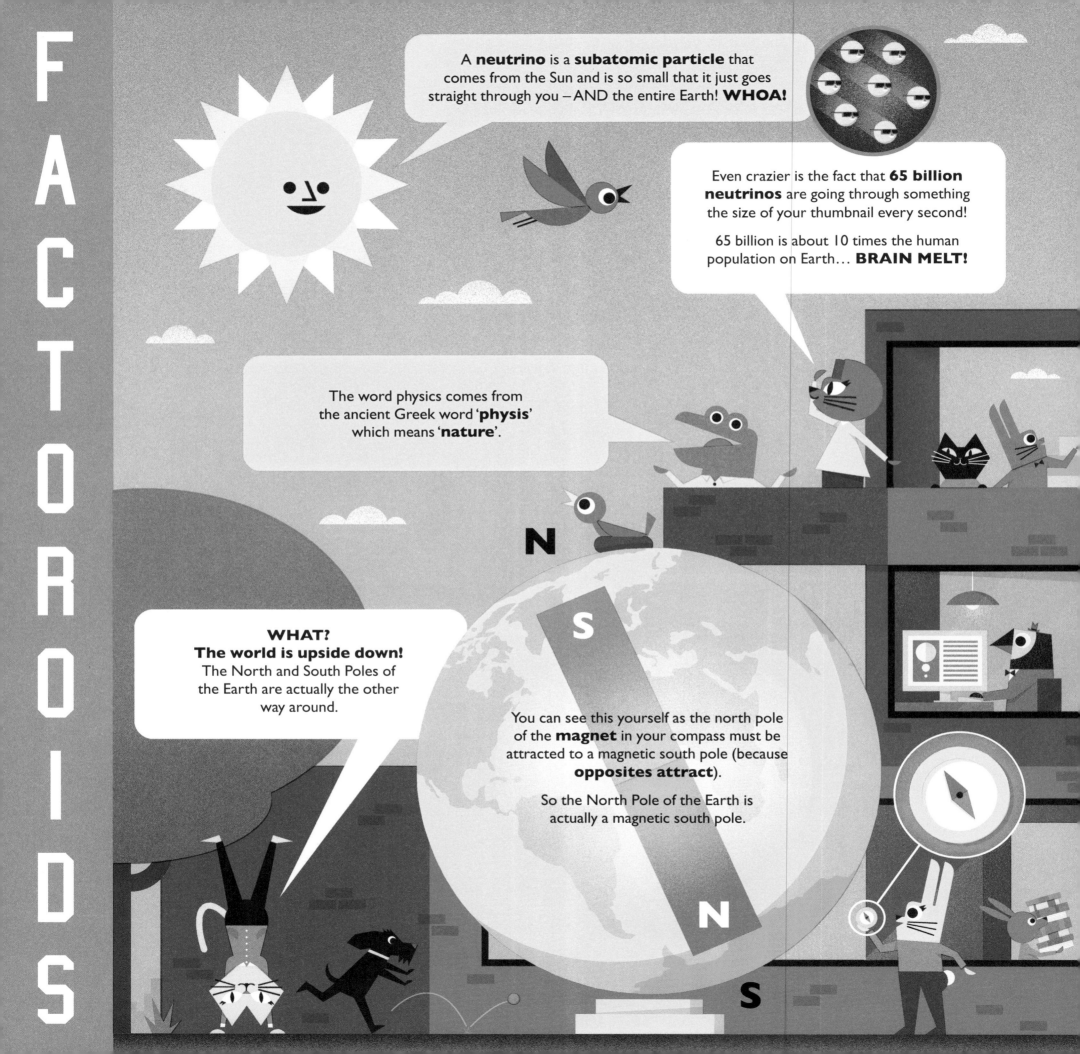

Could I transform my hot dog into a hammer? No, but the **nuclear weak force** lets protons turn into neutrons and vice versa. This allows atoms of one element to turn into another element.

It is a very important part of the **nuclear fusion** that happens in the Sun. **If it wasn't for the nuclear weak force, the Sun wouldn't keep shining!**

ASTRO ★ LABS

All of the protons in the nucleus have a positive electrical charge so they should repel each other and rip apart.

The **nuclear strong force** acts like a gravity so incredibly strong that it **keeps the nucleus of an atom together.**

Wow, what an adventure! Science has helped us discover a huge amount about the Universe but it seems that the more we learn, the more questions we uncover. **Will we ever understand everything there is to know? Is it possible to fully understand the Universe?**

Nobody knows! But there is only one way to find out: keep exploring! We'll need lots of friends out there to probe the edges of science. Who knows, perhaps you'll be the next person to help solve one of the great mysteries of the Universe!

KNOWLEDGE AWAITS!

GLOSSARY-INDEX

Magnetism *42-43*
A fundamental property of particles.

Mass *8-9, 22-23, 30-31, 34-35, 52-53, 58-59*
How much matter something is made of.

Mathematics *58-59*
A set of logical rules that describes things in physics really well.

Matter *22-23, 30-31, 48-49, 58-59*
Anything that takes up space and has mass.

Measurement *8-9, 22-23*
An accurate way of explaining the size, length or amount of something.

Metamaterial *50-51*
A material that is made to control light in an interesting way.

Metre (m) *8-9*
The standard unit of measurement.

Minute *8-9*
60 seconds

Mixture *18-19, 20-21*
More than one chemical compound mixed up but not bonded together.

Molecule *18-19, 20-21, 24-25, 28-29, 32-33, 40-41, 44-45, 48-49, 50-51, 54*
A collection of several atoms bonded together.

Neutron *12-13, 14-15, 52-53, 54*
A particle carrying no electrical charge, found in the nucleus of atoms.

Nuclear Fission *52-53*
An atom splitting apart into two atoms and releasing energy.

Nuclear Fusion *52-53*
Two atoms joining together to make a new atom and releasing energy.

Nuclear Physics *38-39, 52-53, 55*
The study of the splitting and joining of atoms.

Nucleus *12-13, 14-15, 52-53*
The centre of an atom, made of protons and neutrons

Particle Physics *54, 55*
The study of the fundamental particles of reality.

Periodic Table *14-15, 16-17*
A chart showing all of the different kinds of chemical element.

Potential energy *36-37, 38-39*
The energy due to something's height off the ground.

Power *38-39, 40-41, 52-53*
A measure of the amount of energy flowing per second.

Pressure *28-29, 30-31, 32-33*
How much force is focused into a certain area.

Proton *12-13, 14-15, 40-41, 52-53, 54*
A particle carrying a positive electrical charge, found in the nucleus of atoms.

Quantum Physics *55, 57*
The laws of physics that describe the smallest things in the Universe.

Quark *54*
A particle that protons and neutrons are made of.

Radioactivity *38-39, 48-49, 52-53*
The study of splitting atoms and the energy and particles they produce.

Reflection *44-45*
Light or sound bouncing off a surface.

Refraction *46-47*
Light being bent by a material.

Results *6-7, 8-9*
The measurements from an experiment, used to see if a hypothesis is correct.

Second *8-9, 14-15, 26-27, 32-33, 34-35, 38-39, 40-41, 44-45, 56-57*
The standard unit for measuring time.

Solid *14-15, 16-17, 20-21, 22-23, 24-25, 32-33, 50-51*
A material where the atoms are tightly packed and can't move past each other.

Speed *26-27, 30-31, 34-35, 50-51, 52-53, 56-57*
A measure of how fast something is moving.

Subatomic Particle *52-53, 54*
Anything that is smaller than an atom.

Superposition *55*
The ability of a particle to be in many different states at once.

Temperature *8-9, 14-15, 16-17*
A measure of how hot or cold something is.

Tension *28-29*
Something being stretched apart.

Theory *58-59*
An explanation for why something happens, based on a tested hypothesis.

Time *2-3, 6-7, 8-9, 26-27, 30-31, 32-33, 38-39, 44-45, 54, 55, 56-57*
A measure of things going from the past into the future.

Wave *36-37, 44-45, 46-47, 48-49*
Energy travelling through wobbles.

Wavelength *48-49*
The distance between one wobble and the next in a wave.

Weight *8-9, 28-29, 30-31, 32-33*
How heavy something is on the surface of the Earth when pushed down by gravity.

Use this glossary to help you understand some of the words in this book whilst we hula hoop!

The authors would like to thank:

BEN NEWMAN

Dedicated to a very inspiring friend, Stephen Kerrison.

I'd like to give a special thank you to Colin & Kathy Newman, Claire Newman, Dora Dewsbery, Nico the snoodle, Timmy Booth, Pete Locke, Nick White, The Melvins, Sam Arthur, Harry Gwinner, Harriet Birkinshaw and Camille Pichon for their incredibly valuable help making this book. An extra special super thank you to my good buddies, Dominic Walliman and Alex Spiro.

DOMINIC WALLIMAN

Dedicated to my good friends Rachel Minto and Oliver Davies.

My special thanks go out to Ursula and Nicholas Walliman and all of my family for being wonder-ful, Theodora Geach for her patience and encouragement, to all my physics teachers especially the brilliant Phil Newman who really got me off on the right track. An extra special thanks to Alex Spiro for believing in us and Ben Newman, my brother in arms, who put such a huge amount of work into this book and without whom this would never have happened.

First published in 2016 by Flying Eye Books,
An imprint of Nobrow Ltd. 27 Westgate Street, London, E8 3RL.

Text © Dr. Dominic Walliman and Ben Newman 2016
Illustrations © Ben Newman 2016
Consultant: Jessica Rowson

5 7 9 10 8 6 4

Printed in Latvia on FSC® certified paper.

FSC
www.fsc.org
MIX
Paper from responsible sources
FSC® C002795

ISBN 978-1-909263-60-4

www.flyingeyebooks.com